I Hear With My Eyes

The story of a gifted autistic boy who sees the color of sounds.

Author: Denise Heising

ISBN: 979-8-9936462-2-0

Forward Boldly Press

Email:
ForwardBoldlyPress@gmail.com

Dedication

To Alexandra, Jake, Joseph, and Emmarose, who share the magic of experiencing life through different eyes.

I Hear with My Eyes

Introduction

Synesthesia ...

This is a form of cross-sensory perception, where one sense triggers a perception in another.

An example of synesthesia is seeing a specific color when you hear a sound, such as seeing the color green when you hear a musical note.

Many famous people have or are believed to experience synesthesia, including musicians like Billie Eilish, Pharrell Williams, and Duke Ellington who often perceive sound as color.

Synesthesia is not a disease, but a rare gift.

Chapter 1 — The Boy Who Saw Sound

The Finch house was loud that afternoon. The television yammered in the living room. His uncle's drill buzzed in the garage. The dishwasher rattled in the kitchen. Every clatter, every vibration, every clink of metal against metal burst into bright, overwhelming colors in Joey's mind.

Red from the drill.
Orange from the TV.
Jagged yellow from the dishes.
Too much. Too fast.

He needed out.

He slipped down the hall, past the laundry room, past the coat closet, and opened the door to the sunroom. And there—like an island of quiet—sat his grandmother's old upright piano.

Sunlight spilled across the old ivory keys. The room smelled like lemon polish and old books. Ferns, in their clay pots, drooped over the edges of the windowsill, their leaves green and moist.

Joey exhaled. Inside his mind, the colors settled.

Like a note carried on a melody, he drifted toward the piano. The wood was scratched and worn, one leg was loose, but still supported the piano's weight. To Joey, it looked strong but tender—almost alive.

He touched a key. A soft, warm note rang out, and behind his eyes, a wash of calm yellow bloomed. He pressed it again. Yellow. Quiet. Deep. He smiled slightly.

"I hear with my eyes," he whispered.

The door creaked and split the silence. Joey jumped as he was suddenly pulled back to the present. His mind had been a million miles away in his secret land of sound and color.

"Ah," Nana June said, stepping in with a laundry basket on her hip. "I wondered when you'd come back to your old friend. It's been a while.

"I—I wasn't doing anything," Joey said quickly.

She smiled. "Honey, I've been waiting for someone to play this old piano again."

She set down the basket and sat beside him. The bench squeaked under the weight of two people.

"Go on," she said, nodding at the keys. "Say hello again."

He pressed the yellow note. She closed her eyes. "Always did love that one."

He studied her. "Nana... do notes feel different to you?"

"Sometimes," she said. "Your great-grandfather used to say notes had personalities. He always said the morning sun lived in Middle C."

Joey's heart fluttered. "It looks like sunlight," he whispered.

Nana June opened her eyes. "Looks?"

He froze.

But she didn't scold or laugh. Instead, she asked, "What do you see, Joseph?"

Slowly, carefully, he said, "Colors. In my mind. When I hear sounds."

She studied him—a soft, knowing gaze. "Then you may have inherited the Finch ears."

"The what?"

"The way your great-grandfather heard the world. Different. Beautifully different."

He felt something uncoil in his chest. The noise of the house faded completely.

"Would you like to learn more than what Nana can teach you?" she asked.

He didn't hesitate, "Yes!"

And just like that, everything in Joey's life shifted, quietly and permanently, like the turning of a page. He had something to look forward to- something personal. The simple knowledge that something awaited him was enough to steady his heart and lift his spirit.

Joey was different than most of the middle schoolers he knew. While others filled their days with noise and competition, Joey carried a quiet curiosity that made him notice things others overlooked—the way sunlight pooled in corners, the way a single word could change the rhythm of a conversation. And now, after that subtle turning of the page in his life, he felt something new stirring inside him. It wasn't loud or dramatic, but it was his—something personal to look forward to, a secret promise waiting just beyond the ordinary. He kept

Nana's promise to find a piano teacher at the forefront of his thoughts.

Most people heard sounds. Joey *saw* them. Rain hitting the window was soft purple. Footsteps down the hall were brown circles. A dog barking down the street was a bright, sharp orange.

He wasn't imagining it. He wasn't confused. It was simply the way his brain worked. He had learned a long time ago—people didn't like hearing about it.

When he was six, he told a classmate his singing was "green around the edges." The boy frowned and said Joey was weird. When Joey explained that laughter made pale yellow sparks in his mind, a girl at school said he was lying to get attention. After that, he learned to keep his colors to himself. He listened quietly. He watched carefully. He waited for safe spaces. The piano felt like one. He returned to it after school every day. He played slowly at first—one note at a time, watching the colors flare gently. Then he played small groups of notes. Then chords. The colors blended.

Layered. Shifted. And for the first time, he didn't feel like the surrounding noise was too much. He felt exactly right.

Chapter 2 – Nana's Secret

A few afternoons later, Nana June appeared again as Joey practiced.

She listened for a moment, leaning against the doorframe. "You know," she said, "your great-grandfather used to sit here in this very spot for hours. Drove your great grandmother mad."

Joey chuckled, "What did he do?"

"He said he was making friends with the notes." She stepped closer. "He believed every sound had a story."

Joey's fingers hovered over the keys. "Did he see colors too?"

"Not that he said outright," she answered. "But he talked about the world like someone more than the rest of us."

Joey swallowed. "Nana... can I tell you something?"

"You can always tell me anything."

He explained all the colors, the shapes, the overwhelming noise at school, the way certain sounds hurt, the way others soothed him. How he sometimes felt like his brain wanted to take in the whole world at once. Other times, all he wanted was to fade quietly into the background and disappear.

She put her hand over his. "Joey, that sounds like a gift to me."

"You don't think it's strange?"

"Oh, it's wonderfully strange," she said. "But so are most beautiful things."

He felt his throat tighten—not with sadness, but relief.

"And I want to help you learn," she added. "I found you a real teacher!"

Joey looked at the piano, then back at his grandmother. "Thank you, Nana!"

And she smiled, the soft kind of smile that made even the sharpest colors in his mind settle gently.

Joey wasn't sure what to expect from his first real piano lesson. But he definitely wasn't expecting Mr. Claiborne. He was tall with silver hair. Eyebrows so expressive they seemed to move independently. His shirt was pressed, shoes polished, and he wore reading glasses hanging from a cord around his neck.

When Mr. Claiborne finally spoke, Joey relaxed. His voice was warm and kind.
His words were measured and not hurried.

"Well, young man," he said, placing a hand on the top of the piano, "I am Mr. Claiborne. You must be Joseph?"

"Yes sir," replied Joey, somewhat sheepishly.

"Very nice to finally meet you," said Mr. Claiblorne, "Your grandmother told me a bit about you. Now, let's meet your instrument properly."

He had Joey sit tall, loosen his shoulders, lift his wrists. "The piano is a conversation," Mr. Claiborne said. "Don't shout at it. Speak to it."

Joey tried Middle C.
Yellow.
Calm.
Familiar.

"Good," said Mr. Claiborne. "You feel the weight. That matters."

He taught Joey major and minor scales—up and down, up and down. The colors surged and layered in Joey's mind: green-gold, pale blue, orange, lavender, silver.

"Do you sense anything when you play these?"
Mr. Claiborne asked.

Joey looked carefully at Mr. Claiborne, unsure
of what he was asking, or the answer he was
looking for. Was this a test, a challenge, or a
chance to be understood? The uncertainty
made his voice catch before he could even try
to respond.

The wise teacher could see the confusion on
Joey's face. He continued, "Some students feel
the notes. Some see patterns. Music affects
everyone differently."

Joey nodded without explaining further. For
now, it was enough that someone believed him
capable.

Not strange.
Not irritating.
Not too much.
Just capable.

When the lesson ended, Mr. Claiborne packed
his things and said, "Practice every day.

Music rewards dedication."

"I will," Joey said, and meant it. He returned to the piano the moment the door closed behind the teacher. He pressed the keys again.

Yellow.
Silver.
Blue.
His colors.
His world.

This was only the beginning. Whenever Joey played the weathered piano, Nana's heart warmed with a smile. He treated it as a friend or companion, and his progress was swift.

Chapter 3 – Colors in the Air

By the end of the third week of lessons, Joey had fallen into a rhythm. He hurried home after school. Every day, he dropped his backpack by the sunroom door, sat on the squeaky bench, and let the colors wash through him. Each note was like a small, glowing creature—bright and fluttering, eager to be shaped into something meaningful.

C was yellow.
D was pale green.
E was warm gold.
F was lavender around the edges.
G shimmered blue-silver.
A glowed orange.
B vibrated violet.

He pressed them one by one, watching their colors rise behind his eyes like smoke. When he played chords, the colors layered:

Sunlight yellow with pale green.
Lavender shadows behind silver-blue.
Orange wrapped in violet.

Sometimes the colors surprised him. Sometimes they overwhelmed him. But mostly, they centered him. They helped him feel calm inside- the only part of his day that truly did.

School had been increasingly hard that week. The cafeteria noise twisted into a chaos of jagged colors. The sound of laughter rippled around him—at times including him, at times directed toward him. That hurt. He dropped the ball three times in gym class, drawing unwanted attention, especially from the boys on the baseball team. He forgot to answer a question in math because his mind got stuck on a pattern in the numbers.

His classmates didn't understand him and most didn't try. It seemed like the piano understood, like Nana. When his fingers touched the keys, the notes curled around him like a warm quilt, whispering secrets only he and Nana could hear. Each chord was a conversation, each melody a memory.

When Mr. Claiborne introduced chords, a whole new world began to open for Joey. Major chords burst like a bright firework of blended yellow and silver. Minor chords were deep violet with soft shadows. Diminished chords were jagged and sharp, like broken glass, but interesting. Seventh chords curled like ribbons.

"Music," Mr. Claiborne said, "is emotion in motion."

Joey nodded. "It feels like that."

"You play with intuition, Joseph," the teacher observed. "That is rare."

Joey felt something warm rise in his chest—pride, he thought. Or maybe hope.

That evening, he stayed in the sunroom longer than usual. As moonlight slipped through the windows, the old ivory keys of the piano faintly shined.

He played slowly, watching the colors swirl.

Yellow.
Silver.
Blue.
Lavender.

He felt calmer than he had all week. But something was growing inside him- something he didn't yet have a name for. Perhaps it was a desire to create. It was an unfamiliar longing to shape those colors into something of his own.

It happened late one restless night. The moon hung high over the backyard, casting a pale glow into his room. Joey lay awake, star ng at the ceiling, listening to the faint hum of the refrigerator downstairs and the occasional car passing on the street. But it was the sound of the piano kept drifting through his memory, keeping him from sleep.

He sat up, slipped into his socks, and tiptoed down the hall. The house was quiet. Everyone was asleep.

He opened the sunroom door. The piano was waiting, almost like it knew he'd be there soon. Joey sat, placed his hands on the keys—and felt something spark inside him.

He pressed a single note.
Warm blue.
Then another.
Gold.
Then a third.
Pale green.

He didn't think. He didn't plan. Melody flowed out of him as if it had always lived there, patient for discovery. He moved into chords, letting the colors guide him. He changed one note, then another, shaping the sound, molding the texture, smoothing the pattern. The music curled and wove its way through him, soft but certain.

Time slipped away. When he stopped, he realized he was breathless. He stared at his hands, then at the sheet of paper he'd filled with scribbled notes.

"This one is mine," he whispered. He played it again—softly this time.

Yellow.
Lavender.
Blue.
Gold.

The colors were the same as before, but now they aligned. They felt right. This wasn't just a melody. It was *his* melody. He didn't know it yet, but that song would change everything.

The next day should have been a good one. He had a new melody- a new sense of purpose. The spark inside of him refused to dim. Joey could feel it, and he felt alive.

But school didn't care about sparks.

At lunch, Joey was telling Mia—his friend since kindergarten—about his new piece. He was excited, speaking quickly, describing how the notes "stacked like a glowing staircase."

"What do you mean, glowing?" Mia asked, curious but cautious.

He hesitated. He'd promised himself not to talk about the colors at school. "It's just... how it feels," he said.

But Noah overheard. "Yo!" Noah said, plopping onto the bench. "Is this that laser-color-music thing again?"

Joey stiffened. "It's not—" he began.

"No, seriously!" Noah laughed. "He says he sees sounds. Like he's some kind of superhero."

Several kids at the next table snickered. Joey felt heat rush to his face.

"Cut it out," Mia said sharply.

"I'm just asking!" Noah protested. "I mean… do you, or don't you?"

Joey's heart pounded. He didn't want to lie, but he didn't want to be laughed at either.

"I don't," Joey muttered.

"Ohhhh," a kid said from behind him. "So he made it up."

"That's weird," someone whispered.

The cafeteria colors exploded—sharp reds, jagged whites, swirling oranges. His mind felt full of bees. He stood abruptly, nearly knocking over his tray. "I—I need to go."

He walked out without looking back. Later, in the quiet bathroom stall, he rocked on his toes, trying to calm the storm in his head. His autism made days like this hard—very hard. He didn't always understand people, and they definitely didn't understand him.

That night, he didn't touch the piano. Instead, Joey sat on his bed, staring at the blank wall, feeling the ache of being different.

Nana June knocked softly and sat beside him. "What happened, sweetheart?"

He told her.

She put her hand on his back. "Let people misunderstand," she said, her voice warm. "But don't let them take your colors away."

He inhaled shakily.

"Tomorrow," she added, "the piano will still be waiting."

Chapter 4 — Emma

Emma Rose loved music long before she knew why.

She loved tapping rhythms on the windowsill with her fingers. She loved humming while she read. She loved the way her teacher's voice changed colors when she read aloud in class. Yes—colors.

Emma never told anyone that she saw them. Not her parents. Not her brothers. Not her teachers. Not even her best friend, Danielle. She learned early that people didn't always believe things they couldn't see. Once, in second grade, she told a classmate that the trumpet in the school band "looked like a gold ribbon flying around the room."

The girl had laughed and told everyone. So, Emma stopped talking about it.

That evening marked the autumn recital for Mr. Claiborne's piano students. Emma had been studying piano since she was six years old. Now, in her fourth year, she finally felt confident and was looking forward to the annual event.

It all began with the youngest performers. They dressed in "professional attire" that made them look both dignified and delightfully comical. The audience clapped and cheered them on. After the youngest students finished, the more advanced and older students played. Emma played her piece well. After her bow it was Joey's turn. That night at the recital—when Joey Finch played his original piece—Emma saw something she had never seen before. It was a turning point.

Stars. She saw stars. White, sparkling stars spinning behind her eyes. Not real ones, but she wasn't imagining them either.

They appeared the same way colors always had. Joey's music made her see beauty. Real beauty.

When the performance ended, something in Emma glowed. She found Joey, tugged on his sleeve and whispered the truth: "It looked like stars."

The way Joey looked at her—like he'd found something he didn't know he was missing—made something warm and bright spread in his chest. Could it be... that someone else saw things too?

Sometimes practice time was difficult for Emma to squeeze into her busy day. She asked her mom if she could keep taking piano lessons.

"Are you sure?" her mom asked. "You have soccer, and Girl Scouts, and—"

"I'm sure," Emma said with renewed enthusiasm. She was completely sure. Finally she thought there was someone else who would appreciate and even understand the colors and stars. Because maybe, just maybe, Joey Finch was like her and would understand.

Emma thought back to her first piano lesson with Mr. Claiborne. It was like stepping into a new world. Mr. Claiborne's studio was clean and well organized. The old music books and sheet music smelled like an old smell, a comforting smell. The piano keys gleamed softly in the light on the piano. Emma sat on the bench, her sneakers dangling a little above the floor.

 Mr. Claiborne adjusted his glasses. "Do you have any experience, Emma?"

"No," she admitted. "But I really want to learn."

"Wanting is half the journey," he said gently. "The piano will meet you where you are." He placed her hands on the keys. They felt cool and smooth—alive, almost. "Try Middle C," he said.

She pressed it. A gentle spark of white burst behind her eyes—soft, like powdered sugar drifting through the air. She gasped.

"What is it?" Mr. Claiborne asked.

"Nothing," she said quickly. "Just... pretty. She remembered his smile.

Remembering that first lesson brought Emma back into the present. She felt like the world had opened a tiny secret door just for her. Emma checked the time. If she didn't hurry, she would be late for her piano lesson. She ran to the music center. When she arrived and rushed through the door, she felt a quiet thrill— friendship waiting.

Just inside, leaning against the railing, was Joey Finch. He wasn't smiling exactly, but he wasn't frowning either. His posture was stiff—he looked nervous—but his eyes were curious.

"How was it? The recital, I mean." he asked.

Emma beamed. "Amazing."

"Good," he said, and she thought she saw his shoulders relax a little. "I'm... glad."

It was the beginning of something like a new color—one Emma had never seen before. A friendship color. Soft and bright, like the first glow before sunrise.

Chapter 5 — Quiet Corners

Over the next weeks, Emma and Joey fell into a pattern neither of them planned, but both of them liked. They met at the music center early on Saturday mornings.

Emma's mom teased, "You two are more dedicated than coffee drinkers." Joey's Nana June winked knowingly.

They sat side by side on the piano bench as Joey practiced chords, their shoulders almost touching.

"Try this one," Joey would say, playing a soft lavender minor chord.

Emma would press the same keys. Behind her eyes, lavender swirled.

"Pretty," she whispered.

Joey nodded. "Yeah."

Sometimes they lingered by the rehearsal room at school just to listen to the orchestra warm up.

As they stood near the door, listening to the violins, Emma whispered, "They sound silver."

"Silver with a little blue," Joey added.

Their eyes met. They smiled—small, secret smiles. This was their world.

One afternoon in March, they found an empty corner practice room at the music center. There was an upright piano inside, a window overlooking the parking lot, and enough space for two to breathe comfortably.

"This could be ours," Emma said.

"Like a hideout," Joey agreed.

"Or a club," Emma said. "A two-person club. Membership requirements: must hear music differently."
 "And must not tell anyone else," Joey acded.

Emma nodded. "Deal."

They shook hands—awkwardly but sincerely. In that tiny practice room, their friendship deepened. They played games like "Name That Chord Color" and "Guess the Rhythm Shape." They didn't have to explain themselves to each other. They didn't have to pretend to be typical. They were simply Joey and Emma. Perfectly different and for the first time, perfectly understood.

"Did you hear the announcements and school yesterday?" Emma looked at Joey with curiosity.

Joey grinned, "You mean when the intercom crackled and I saw orange spiderwebs?"

"Me too!" laughed Emma. "Principal Dawes said that this year's Spring Talent Showcase is May 19th. Sign-ups are now posted outside the office!" Emma sat up straighter.
She knew this could be big—huge—for Joey.
For herself, too.

"I really hadn't thought about it," Joey admitted. "Let's talk tomorrow. Right now, it's time to head home—my stomach's growling."

Emma chuckled at the rumble, "See you tomorrow, Joey."

The following day, Emma caught Joey at his locker. "Joey," she said breathlessly, "we should do something for the talent show."

He blinked. "Like what? Magic tricks?"

"No!" she laughed. "A duet."

"A... piano duet?"

"Yes!" Her eyes sparkled. "Our two styles together. Mr. Claiborne can help us pick a piece—or we can mash up our melodies.

Joey stared at the floor. His fingers twitched. His breath came faster. "Emma, I... I don't do well with crowds."

"I know," she said gently. "But I'll be there. We can be brave together."

He didn't answer. She waited. Finally, he whispered, "Maybe."

That was all she needed.

The next day, Joey felt off. Not bad, exactly—but scrambled. Tangled. He kept thinking about the talent show and about Emma. About doing something new. Something bold. The cafeteria laughs came back to him—sharp and muddy-colored.

After school, Emma met him in their corner practice room. "You seem quiet," she said softly.

"I'm always quiet," he muttered.

"No," she said, shaking her head. "This is different-quiet."

Joey pressed his thumb into the piano bench fabric, trying to find words. Eventually, they slipped out, small and hard. "People at school think I'm weird."

Emma's face softened. "Why?"

Joey hesitated. Then... trust won. "Because I'm autistic." He waited for her to flinch. Or look confused. Or make one of those pity faces.

But she simply said, "Okay. What does that mean for you?"

No one had asked him that before. "It means the world is loud," he said quietly. "And confusing sometimes. I don't always understand jokes. And noise hurts. And people don't like that I'm bad at sports. And sometimes I don't know what to say."

Emma nodded thoughtfully. "That must be really hard."

He looked up, startled. No one had ever said that either.

"I think your brain is beautiful," she added softly. "It helps you see music in ways I can't."

Joey's throat tightened. "Thank you," he whispered.

Emma smiled. "So… duet?"

Joey breathed out slowly. "Yes," he said. "Duet."

Their hands brushed as they began to play. Two sets of fingers. Two different brains. Two hearts learning to speak the same language.

Chapter 6

Building Something Beautiful

For the next two weeks, Emma and Joey worked on their duet every day after school— sometimes in the sunroom at Joey's house, sometimes in their practice room at the music center. Nana's smile glowed as bright as the sun. Watching the children grow and learn was a gift beyond measure.

It wasn't easy, at least not at first. Joey liked structure. He wanted a plan, a pattern, a roadmap. Emma liked improvisation. She enjoyed adding little sparkles and twists to melodies. Their first attempts were messy.

"You're playing too fast," Joey complained.

"You're playing too slow," she countered. "And that part is too loud."

 "Well, yours is too soft," Joey huffed.

They glared at each other over the piano keys. Then, slowly... something shifted. They learned to listen. Really listen.

Joey began to understand Emma's rhythms. She liked to float above the melody, to sprinkle shimmer on top. Emma learned that Joey's part was the foundation—the steady earth beneath her sky. Soon, their music didn't clash. It merged.

One evening, Mr. Claiborne walked into their practice room unexpectedly. He stood quietly in the doorway, listening as their duet unfolded. When they finished, out of breath and grinning, he wiped his glasses. "My dears," he said thoughtfully, his eyes shining, "that is real music."

Emma looked at Joey. Joey looked at Emma. They both felt it too. Something real was forming.

The week before the talent show, something unexpected happened at school. Joey was heading to math class when Noah jogged up beside him. "Hey—Joey. Can we talk?"

Joey stopped. His stomach lurched. "Why?" he asked stiffly.

Noah shifted awkwardly, rubbing the back of his neck. "Look... I wanted to say I'm sorry."

Joey blinked. "For what?"

"For laughing at you. For the cafeteria stuff. For being a jerk."

Noah was sincere. Joey was too stunned to speak.

"Emma explained some things to us," Noah said. "About how you hear music. And about... you know... being autistic." His voice softened.

"I didn't get it. But I want to try." Joey stared. Noah swallowed nervously. "And… uh… everyone says your talent show piece is gonna be amazing. I hope I can hear it."

Joey didn't know what to say. His throat felt tight. But he managed, "Thanks." And he meant it. He could tell that the apology from Noah wasn't easy.

As Noah walked away, Joey felt something bright inside him—something that wasn't anger or fear. Something like sunrise.

Joey practiced with renewed confidence. When he told Emma about Noah's apology, she smiled. She could see that something inside Joey had shifted— a change for the better.

Chapter 7 — The Talent Show

The auditorium buzzed with excitement. Decorations hung across the stage. Microphones hummed. Parents filled the rows, waving at their children. Performers paced backstage, whispering lines and practicing dance steps.

Joey's heart hammered in his chest.

Emma took his hand. "You okay?"

"No," he said honestly. "But... better because you're here."

Emma squeezed his fingers. "Let's be brave together."

The piano was wheeled into place. Their names were called. They stepped onto the stage. Lights warmed their faces. The audience quieted. Joey saw the blur of teachers, students, parents—and in the very front row... Noah. He was already standing and applauding!

Joey inhaled sharply.

Ready?" Emma asked softly, leaning close.

"As I'll ever be." Joey breathed, his reply quiet but steady.

They sat at the piano. Emma played the first note. It was a soft, sparkling white. Joey answered with a deep violet chord. The duet began.

Their hands danced across the keys. Emma's high, twinkling notes floated like stars. Joey's rich, steady chords grounded everything with warmth and depth. Their styles blended— two different worlds forming one breathtaking sound.

The auditorium changed. Whispers stopped. Laughter died. Everyone listened. Even the football players in the back row leaned forward. The members of the baseball team, who had teased Joey earlier in the year, watched with wide, quiet eyes.

Halfway through, their hands crossed on the keys, a perfect knot of motion and trust. Joey felt something surge in his chest. A new color— one he'd never felt before—gold and blue and silver woven together. The color of courage.

When the final note faded, there was a heartbeat of silence. Then, a roar. Applause thundered through the auditorium. Kids stood. Teachers clapped.

Someone shouted, "Encore!"

Emma turned to Joey, breathless with joy. "They saw it," she whispered.

Joey shook his head, smiling through tears. "They saw *us*."

The crowd was still cheering when Emma whispered, "They want another song."

Joey swallowed. "What should we play?"

Emma looked at him, eyes shining, "Yours." His moonlight melody. His first real creation. The piece that made him feel brave for the first time. Joey nodded. They repositioned their hands. The crowd hushed immediately.

He pressed the first note—yellow. Then blue. Then green. Emma joined him, adding scft harmonies that curled like silver smoke. Together, they played his piece—not as two musicians, but as two friends who understood each other in a way the rest of the world rarely did.

As the last note drifted into silence, Joey realized something: his autism didn't make him less. It made him different, and that difference made his music possible. Made his friendship with Emma possible. Made this moment possible.

When the applause rose again—louder than ever—Joey didn't shy away. He embraced it; all of it. There were tears on his face, and on Emma's. When they looked at each other they laughed gentle laughs and smiled big smiles.

This was the first time that Joey could remember being appreciated by his peers and even teachers. There was a newfound respect and acceptance for him and his struggles. The ache left by years of cruel jokes seemed to vanish. Emma knew it too. Her heart lifted. She had never seen Joey so happy.

Epilogue — Two Notes, One Song

Summer arrived slowly, with warm mornings and firefly evenings. Emma and Joey spent many of those days in the practice room, creating new music together. They laughed, argued about chord progressions, invented silly harmony games, and sometimes just sat quietly, listening to the world outside.

Emma looked at Joey one afternoon as sunlight painted the piano keys golden. "You know," she said, "we should make an album someday."

Joey snorted. "Of what? Us arguing?"

She laughed. "No, us making music. You and your colors. Me and my sparkles."

He thought for a moment. Then nodded. "Yeah. We could."

Their friendship was steady now. It was as solid as a chord that felt just right. Sometimes kids at school still didn't understand them. Sometimes the world was loud and confusing. But Joey wasn't alone anymore.

Emma wasn't either. Together, they made a world of notes and colors—real, honest, beautiful. And even though they were only in middle school, one thing was clear: This was just the beginning of their music.

A new melody.
A new color.
A new story.
One they would write together.

9 798993 646220